Five Minute Reads and Self Discovery

BY

Meera Niharika Vyas

ISBN 978-93-5438-390-8

Published in India 2020 by Pencil

A brand of
One Point Six Technologies Pvt. Ltd.
123, Building J2, Shram Seva Premises,
Wadala Truck Terminal, Wadala (E)
Mumbai 400037, Maharashtra, INDIA
E connect@thepencilapp.com
W www.thepencilapp.com

Author biography

Meera Niharika Vyas is an author of Dear Future Husband.

Connet:- Vyasmeera3@gmail.com

Instagram:- @meeraniharikavyas

Let them sleep in your garage.

Keep your eyes open while driving. Say NO to noisy crackers.

Make communities and collect funds for their vaccination (for your safety).

Don't limit your humanity over a specific breed or class.

Connect:-

Vyasmeera3@gmail.com

https://instagram.com/meeraniharikavyas?igshid=7bzry4rgpgwh

@meeraniharikavyas

"Sooner or later we all discover that the important moments in life are not the advertised ones, not the birthdays, the graduation, the weddings, not the great goals achieved. The read milestones are less prepossessing. They come to the door of memory unannounced, stray dogs that amble in, sniff around a bit and simply never leaves. Our lives are measured by these."

—Susan B. Anthony

Contents

Introduction

I've summed up my twenty five years in five chapters, and trust me it's not just my story, but yours. You just need to open your eyes and observe your life. We all have so different yet similar stories. Life has different phases, we all go through those, knowingly or unknowingly. High school insane fun phase. Craziness for that favorite actor phase. That first die hard crushing and heart-break phase. First hostel phase. And then harsh the real world phase.......Read these five phases of life in five chapters.

Are you wondering about the most important phase...The soulmate phase? Of course, but partners never settle in one chapter—they need a book. They deserve a book. They deserve a book series.

Do check my book *Dear Future Husband* on Amazon.com :-
www.amazon.com/dp/B08R8Y3T66

Kindle edition on Amazon.in:-
https://wwwamazon.in/dp/B08R7X1SW3/ref=cm_sw_r_wa_apa_yC35FbTK6TXW8

The second part of the book deals with self awareness and self acceptance, answer the given questions and figure out how much you know yourself. Then answer all the questions and know the best version of yourself. Checkout the major bucket list and not to do lists.

1.

Fanatical

It takes a lot in being a fan!

Our parents got the finest age of TV; shows like Buniyad, Mahabharata, Fauji, Sarkar Ki Duniya, Alif Laila, Ramayana, Pradhanmantri, Mungerilal ke Haseen Sapne , Malgudi days, Byomkesh Bakshi, Bharat Ek Khoj, and Chitrahaar weren't just critically praised but they prepared their viewers to think.

By the time our generation started watching television, either all the good shows were dusted, or we started watching television at a very early age—I fit to the second class, I started watching TV too early— Office Office, Shriman Shrimati, Sarabhai V/s Sarabhai, Family no. 1, Hum Panch, Shakalaka Boom Boom, Shararat, Tu Tu Main Main , repeats of Mahabharata, Ramayana and Shaktimaan molded my mind in such a way that I built up a tendency to study everything around me. Television gives insight to the community. It plays a very vital part in mental evolution; you don't realize it while watching the show but they are mirrored in your humor, your personality, and your style of thinking.

I've seen TV dying in front of my eyes, but let's not go there. I'm here to talk on how TV changed my life fully when I was a child. And the program that got me obsessively addicted was not the one with 8-9 ratings, it was a mere 3 starrer, shitty soap opera. Now, I'm overly critical over any show or book or movie, but still when I put on that soap opera, I quite get carried away.

The show gripped me in such a way that I fell in love with some characters. It introduced me to the notion of fandom. As time passed, I followed more shows (better ones) and in no time I grew into an impassioned fan of Amit Sadh, Surveen Chawla, Jennifer Winget and of course, Fawad Afzal Khan.

Fifteen years back I had no friends, I was boring — annoying girl who didn't talk funny, who didn't score well.

Then when television came into my life, I turned into the schoolgirl who watches serials; my teachers criticized me, my classmates gave me that judgy look of being a bad influence. But in the process I found some people who were just like me. And for the first time in my school life or in my overall life, I became friends with girls who celebrated me for who I am. I had friends with whom I could have fun, not just the one with whom I can have my tiffin in the recess. I never knew a soap opera could give me friends for life. In no time, I became lively and upbeat, my scores improved remarkably, math became my favorite subject. Though I could never join the geeky zone as the stamp of being the soap opera girl remained.

My obsessiveness for my favorite artists was seeking me a lot of attention between family, friends, and at school. When I chose to give up watching that soap opera, people considered that as a serious subject. Some even specifically visited me, nobody ever visited me before. Specifically.

Well I stopped watching the show, but the show stayed inside. From an obsessed viewer I developed into an obsessed fan. It was cool by the time I was in school, but as we entered our senior year, where girls chatted about guys, dates and sex; I still talked about Amit Sadh, Surveen Chawla, and Jennifer Winget. Few years later, when Zindagi aired, Fawad Khan entered the list and topped it. Ah! Fawad <3.

That was a tough year, I swapped my studies for the board examination with binge watching Dastan, Humsafar and ZGH. And still managed to pull off a respectable 92%. This must sound good, but it was worse than failing. Because of this score, I started speculating that my obsession is not harming me in any way and I'm a genius.

By the end of 2016, I was so obsessed with the four of them that I had to take gap years as I failed in my medical entrance. That year I noticed that my obsession and day dreaming is actually OCD. I told my parents that I want to get out of all this, but deep in my core I knew, the moment I'll get over them, I'd be all alone and depressed like I was in my early school days.

Today when I saw this old poem that I wrote in four years back, the journey I painted in these four years, wrestling against my own mind, flashed in front of my eyes-

"From past ten years, the sun shines a little brighter while the stars seem to lose their light.

I've been doing a lot of insanity from collecting their pictures, writing their dialogues to some huge family fights.

Whenever I decide to stop day dreaming and focus on my life, they'd invades my thoughts as a morning dream;

And won't leave till the moment I go back to sleep.

Ruining one more day I had planned for my exams,

But still I'd tell myself, I'm left with another back-up plan.

Even in the worse days and the hardest time, when I find myself alone after a paroxysm,

Their thoughts as soothing as the morning light, always helping me get through the sleepless nights.

These are the things that make obsession such a blissful game,

I always hope no medicine could heal me ever, as with them there is not even the slightest pain.

Hey but being a fan is not this light.

Every day the sun sets, I lay down in bed and the harsh reality kisses me good night.

Leaving me with the regret that one more day is off,

Outlying me from the race of being on the top.

My friends tell me I should get over them because we're no more in school.

And I always reply with a smile, they're the antidepressants that keep me cool.

No matter what I do or say, the core of my heart knows what I believe in is a big lie,

One more year is gone and I'm still in the same mess making myself regret with a sigh.

2.

Little Heaven

The journey of "I don't like school, I want to work," to "I don't like to work I want to go back to school,".

The bright world outside the school gate that always fascinated us deals with drugs, depression, assaults, inequality, materialism and practicality.

Dear Carmelites

The roller-coaster ride of emotions that I encounter every time I visit Carmel is something beyond words, beyond anything. These boundaries have willingly or unwillingly protected us from the harsh world of superior and inferior, for more than 12 years.

Yes, everything changed over years but uncountable memories, adventures, lessons, friends and of course stories. This building gave me and all of us will always be immortal and pure, probably the purest. Being an insensitive person, I never thought on the first day that I'd cry so much in the last month, and never in my nightmares had I imagined the hardship of life to be beyond school politics, suspension, compartments and the day when all your friends are absent.

To the days where those diary remarks and incomplete home works seemed the biggest tragedy of life. Where the only required revolution was annual function's non filmy classics and allowance to wear casuals on children's day. The anxious sleepless nights were just the outcome of our excitement before the much awaited birthday celebration at school, the thrill of distributing chocolates in the staff room, dilemma of choosing the favorite friend to walk around the whole building and the chaos of increasing the budget for throwing lavish parties at the *chaat* stall outside. When egg rolls and expensive ice cream were the only representative of economic inequalities.

I can still picture myself running down the corridor with my friends giggling and bitching, suddenly freezing to silence the moment Miss Rina Fernandez was heard in her South Indian English accent—chilling.

We may have different hangout places now, more fancy and cool, but my eyes still search for the campus washrooms, the dirty heavens where none of us were pretending, where the most serious discussions didn't include social taboos but geography paper and coaching crush.

Walking around freely in the campus was dreadful, but the threats were not the fear of being raped, robbed or thrown acid at, instead the diary remarks and suspension.

We've seen India in our auditorium, Independence Day, *Rangoli* competition, Christmas plays. The real essence still was the politics, oath ceremony of some deserving and some non-deserving cabinet ministers. But my favorite was walking behind the red curtain on stage.

The new constructions were not to record their active tenure but a necessity, our new basement was the necessity of our lunch breaks especially during morning classes where every steps were counted on the needles of school clock (wrist watches were not allowed) by the time you walk under the Ashok tree at the end of the field, tannah! Break is over. Basements acted as a savior, it undoubtedly witnessed the most dramatic birthday parties ever. The heart of the campus. We could keep our eyes on everything happening around without being noticed.

The way to library flickers me with the glimpse of how hard we tried to maintain pin drop silence,

Well, the fact that school libraries are for self-study still leaves me confused, it's like politicians are for wellbeing for the country.

I loved bragging that my school had the biggest playground that gave us numerous cricket and kabaddi matches, our self-defense classes were just a throwaway period that time, but now I think I have threatened a lot of people with "I'm a blue belt".

Fandom is a necessity, the 2012 batch was the most famous batch in terms for being the role models in fields other than just academics. And that wasn't my batch, we were the fans. The followers.

Carrying the glorifying tag of being the worst batch ever, our classroom still echoes with all the chaos and hassle. We yelled, laughed, fought, some even cried, but hiding emotions were not the trend then. We were alive. We were expressive, we were less damaged.

And no matter how much annoying and partial our teachers were, the fact cannot be denied that they somewhat succeeded in intentionally or unintentionally molding us into beautiful teenagers, not just academically. While we were breathing secularism, equality, patriotism and spirituality, the world outside the campus kept on struggling to even get the right definition.

I remember my idea of castes, as the history teacher taught us "People divided on the basis of the work they do" with no pre assumed opinion added, by the age I was 16, I never realized it was a taboo, she didn't say being shudra was assumed inferior. We never thought that. We were taught to look up at every individual, every work with dignity, labors day was one of the best celebrations we had. We were supposed to clean our classroom, the playground, the basement all by ourselves, and it didn't seem shameful or offensive at all.

The only stereotype change seen back then was an easy going cute principal of missionaries. Who never scolded anyone or dragged things beyond the line. At least my school was not a reflection of that brutality.

Carmel and its stories are not something to be finished off in one chapter or even a book, every day, every period, every assembly, every duty and every break is a collection of uncountable memories, even our tiny overcrowded school buses could write novels on itself.

I wonder when time flew, and we grew up (at least physically and by age) leaving behind our school. Carmel was my little version of heaven, whose memories always leaves me nostalgic. And heartbroken, when I see people for what they have become are after leaving school.

I wish we become an important part of the change the society needs, bringing into practice all the important lessons we learnt during our school days, not just when they were teaching.

Your Fellow Schoolmate.

Meera

3.
We Forget

Women die, trends change, and we forget.

We concentrate on their dresses, their accent, their last calls, their work, their body, their character, their age, their religion.

We think on how many fake rape cases are reported, how me too india is injustice to men.

And how we should concentrate on #NotAllMen"

We discuss victim and culprit's religion. [To clear the misinterpretation, victim is the one who has been raped and culprit is the one who raped.]

If the girl survives, we leave no opportunity to make her life hell because she was raped. They didn't rape her, she was raped. Files will multiply, but no real justice will ever prevail. Because even now, we have our reasons to play the religion game, to play the character game, the gender game. The case has to be the rarest of rare cases, because clearly rape is not rare. The culprit should be adult enough to get punished. So what if he raped someone at fourteen or sixteen!

Someone is raped and we couldn't get over the trauma of how media sympathizes rapists of a particular community, how the victims of another community are neglected. We talk according to the community's comfort zone or the gender's comfort zone or maybe our generation's comfort zone.

I live in a system where people quarrel among themselves when a girl or person is raped. For men it's even worse, when a man is raped, people LAUGH.

What further does unity ask for to demand justice? And to clarify again by justice I mean, justice of that girl or that person, not religious justice or caste justice or any political justice. Justice where it's absolutely a crime to rape, not just a social media crime and no matter if it's among a rarest case or not, the criminal must die....soon.

We're a crowd of impostors, who don't care about other's misfortune. Deep down each one of us is terrorized, what if tomorrow it's our turn, we repress that voice with a louder character assassination—why was she dressed that way? Why was she out so late? Why was she friends with that man? Why did she ignore that man? It might sound like the girl is being questioned, but in reality, we're consoling our heart. I won't wear that dress, so I won't be raped. I won't go out late, so I won't be raped, I won't talk to a man, so I won't be raped, I won't ignore a man, so I won't be raped.

Society, you will be raped if you keep on justifying it, because dresses don't rape, timing doesn't rape, your behavior doesn't rape, THE RAPIST RAPES.

People hoot in the theater, when the main lead gives rape threat to a woman, that's heroic? I hear justification like 'the lady (in the movie) was cheating on her husband, so she deserved rape treat.'

I never knew punishment to defraud is rape. Is there a retribution for marital rape?

The women objectifying songs are time's choice, not just the men of our generation, but even the women love these songs where they are treated like a sex toy.

Our frequent conversations have lines like *"Woh kare toh mazak, hum karein toh balatkaar,"*

These are our everyday contribution to 'Rape Culture'. And suddenly when justice for the rape victim is trending, we turn into the most conscientious citizen on social media.

Now, that is our everyday contribution to hypocrisy.

Do you get goosebumps when you read the word Rape? Not just when it's trending, but in normal lives?

Even when it's the most common crime, even when 90% children and women are being or have been sexually victimized, nobody speaks out, nobody let them speak out.

It goes on every day, every hour. And we more or less don't care. We laugh at rape jokes! Hoot at rape threats, dance at such songs.

People protest for women, then in our speeches we use lines like 'Haath mein Churiya pehen rakhi hai?'

We post a lot on social media, abusing the rapists or molesters, how do we exactly abuse — 'Behen**od Ma****od.' But that's the new cool, People on social media have millions of fans because of this.

And after a few weeks or less, we will eventually forget...

4

Crushes and co.

I love my life, not that I'm privileged or I've not seen hardship, but I love my life because of the people I have around me, my family, some random good people, and a few friends.

I love my life because I know I'm god's one favorite children (if not the only favorite child

I love my life because in spite of all the situations I have been in, I came out of those, all by myself, as a much stronger and better person.

I have been sexually assaulted for eight years (like any other girl or child probably, I've been in depression for seven years. There have been points where I had no one to talk, where I was all alone crying in one corner of my room. When my four years relationship ended, I felt like there's nothing left in the world, I was vulnerable, and I was alone. I had an emotional breakdown when I visited Kashmir and heard them. The inhumanity around the world had me at the edge, and I felt like I'm so helpless to not change it.

I came out of all this as a better person, learning what I was supposed to.

In my twenty-five years of life, hardship came as a time of testing and I passed (more or less).

But that one phase of life, when I had a crush on this guy in my senior year, my first teenage crush that is supposed to be cute and adorable. It was not. It turned into a nightmare that haunts me still.

He made me feel like the ugliest and the dumbest girl on this entire planet, and I kind of started believing that. My accent, my face, my texts, my walk, my dresses, my every single action was a subject to laugh on. I was a joke.

For my seven years younger and tender heart, that phase and the terms I was referred by, were shocking. That was the first time I visited a psychiatrist.

I've been almost raped, I've suffered numerous mental illness, serious break up and many failures, but those two years of humiliation still top the list of my worst living nightmares. That was my first encounter with real insecure world, whose pride depended on other's disgrace.

Dear Ex Crush and co.

I reached out to you in the hope that by this point you must have attained a mental maturity to realize your wrongdoings, but as most do, you didn't.

You will never understand that the way you treat others is not a reflection of them, it is a reflection of you.

You will never realize that the words you pin to a specific person just to get some attention in your circle, affect them. You will never see that the way you mock people does not go unnoticed, even if it's done behind the back of that person.

I refuse for the way you treat people to make my heart cold. I still ask for your whereabouts and apologize for treating you 1/20th of how you treated me.

I will not allow for myself to dislike you so much that I hate you, because I am not the type of person that hates others. I love others.

I want you to know that, despite the mean and hurtful things you have done to me, just to be cool, I forgive you. You are too shallow to apologize, but god has blessed me with enough spirituality to hear my soul, I forgive you. I hope the world shows you nothing but goodness and love and realization of your deeds. I know you are not aware that the things in this life that are the most worthwhile are moments that you share with people in times of pure and honest joy, because you're not pure and honest, not to others, not to yourself.

I hope you get the strength and virtue to introspect, because karma has its own harsh way.

You are not the first group who seek validations by putting others down, and I am sure you will not be the last. I do know, however, that you are the last one that will ever affect me.

5

City of Academic Dreams

Dear Kota,

As the weather and the world are unpredictable from a few months, my mother was keeping records of all the umbrellas we have at home. There I found this green and black umbrella with ALLEN, written in bold. Our grey suit and white dupatta flashed in front of my eyes, taking me on a magnificent trip to nostalgia. I'm sitting in my bedroom, the room that knew all my childhood wishes and nightmares. You were always a nightmare. I grew up wishing for a comfortable and average life with no survival struggle—like the other people I know, who spend their lives on expensive gadgets and at least in an air conditioned flat. I now sit here thinking about how different my life is now and how much better it is from the life I imagined in my childhood. And for that, I am thankful to you as well.

As cliché as it sounds, you completely changed me as a person. Starting out, I was a terrified, homesick girl, overprotective about my gadgets and space. From there when I moved to your state, I didn't even get to pack my world, leaving behind things without which I never imagined myself surviving even for one complete hour. My Phone and My Laptop. Leaving behind my room, my bathroom and my pampering family, I headed to the city of academic dreams.

You contributed in making me a grown up, you gave me my first hostel life, forcing me to be responsible on my own. You took me in as a girl who barely realized the worth of whatever she had in life, who barely knew how to wake up on her own, who often missed her school bus for extra nap, you made her wake up for 4am yoga, 5am self-study and 6am class without any reminder. When I went for grocery shopping for the first time and spent not a penny more than what I needed, you taught me value for money. When the *mess wale bhaiya* didn't shift my luggage from ground floor to third floor for free, and I had to do it by my own, my past 18 years flashed in front of my eyes. When I yelled at my servants for not getting me a glass of water, which was barely ten steps away from me. You taught me the value of people. After the sixteen hours of hard work, you gave me the best sleep, in that cooler—the sleep that I never experienced at home, at the 22 degrees of air conditioner.

You were the first to give me the chance to meet people from all over the country and call some of those my friends. Let me tell you, you have got the sweetest and the most helpful people ever. When the shopkeeper didn't stop me from taking the spiral notebook, even when I had ten rupees less. When the shops exchanged things, I bought two months back without any frustration. When my classmates cleared all my doubts without judging me to be weak or dumb. When my leg was fractured and a stranger helped me without even knowing me. Your people taught me the beauty of being a good person. You gave me opportunities that I never had back at home, you made me accept my Bihari accent, my no makeup face, the loud and quirky me, without any hesitation. You made me realize that when I accept myself the way I am, people will do the same. I am a different person, a better person, a more determined and happier person. I know what I want and I'm not afraid to go after it. I'm not afraid of failing anymore, I'm not afraid of falling short or even being rejected. I'm confident in the person I've become and the person I will turn into.

In eight months, I got enough memories to fill my diary, though I don't have a single picture for the photo albums, no slams or ODs. We girls who used to bump into each other's room at three in the morning to clear our doubts, we are not even in touch anymore. But I'm sure, just like me, each of us have enough stories for our children. And oh, the new year's night, although we belonged to a low budget hostel and we didn't have those lavish parties with loudspeakers and good food, but the owner managed to treat us with ice cream and *golgappa* . We treated ourselves with the most delicious cheese burger of this world form a local burger shop. And full night high stereo music, from that broken music system of hostel's second hand van. That was one of the best nights ever. The big city nights are not even close to the fun we had at our damaged yet the most peaceful and happy terrace.

've read many books and heard a lot of stories about successful and hardworking people, but you made me witness those. My classmates used to set different examples for me, they never gave up—not in jaundice, not in malaria, NEVER. Nothing stopped them.

Those suicide months around January and March were super scary for my parents, one girl committed suicide next to my hostel that was shocking. Teachers used to travel hostel to hostel to motivate us and prevent as much suicides as they could, but when you have fourteen to twenty lakh aspirants for barely five thousand seats, you cannot avoid suicide, but media and government can hide the news.

In spite of the suicides, you won my trust, the trust that no human could ever earn. At four in the morning, I could walk on the road fearlessly, I could walk from all those vacant lanes without horror, and I could be on the van or auto alone, without my cellphone, with no worries. I never needed to lock my room before leaving. Even in the water crisis, those unhygienic food, those big rats and mosquitoes, I was satisfied and at peace, because you taught me 'you get what you put in' and I was putting in a lot of honesty, dedication and hard work.

Thank you Kota, Thank You for everything. Even after so many years nothing faded. Never in my life can I forget you.

To Know Yourself-1

"Knowing yourself is the begining of all wisdom"

-Aristotle

1.What is your DREAM LIFE? And why? In Details.

2. What does happiness mean to you?

3.Who is your biggest inspiration? Why?

4. If you had a super power, what would it be? And Why?

5. What are your three wishes and Why? In Details.

6.What is your next five years plan? Where do you wanna be in life?

7.What is your PASSION? What do you REALLY wanna do? And Why?

8. Five things that make you the happiest? Why?

9.What are all the things you are thankful for? (Even the little things)

10. Top 10 priorities of your life?

11.5 things you are good at?

12.5 things you love about yourself?

13. 5 things you wanna change about yourself?

14. Top 5 goals of one year.

15. What is missing in your life right now?

16. Are you happy? Yes or No? And Why? In details.

17. Five most important people in your life?

18.What are you afraid of? Why?

19.How can you show more love and compassion to your most important people, every day?

20. How can you improve your daily routine?

21. What is your daily routine? Present and Improved.

22. What is spirituality?

23. What is your mental and emotional goal for this year?

24. What is your physical goal?

25. What is your idea of a happy life? In details.

26. What is your idea everyday of self-care?

28. What do you wanna change in the society? How?

100 Things To Do Before You Die-

Highlight what you have already done. Add what's not in the list.

1. LEARN TO DRIVE

2. GET INTO A COLLEGE

3. FIGURE OUT WHAT YOU WANNA DO IN LIFE

4. FALL IN LOVE

5. GET A JOB

6. GET MARRIED

7. MAKE SNOW ANGEL

8. DANCE IN RAIN

9. KISS UNDER THE BRIDGE OF SIGH

10. EARN GOOD WHITE MONEY

11. LIVE IN A HOUSEBOAT

12. GO TO AN ISLAND

13. GO ON SAFARI

14. HAVE A CHILD\

15. HAVE A PARENTING PLAN
16. DONATE BLOOD
17. BECOME AN ORGAN DONAR
18. OWN A PET
19. BUY YOUR OWN HOUSE
20. GO ON A ROAD TRIP WITH FRIENDS
21. GO TREKKING WITH BAE
22. GO ON A LUXURIOUS TRIP WITH FAMILY
23. CREATE YOUR DREAM HOME
24. PROPOSE ON A HOT AIR BALLOON
25. RIDE A LIMO
26. CELEBRATE ALL FESTIVALS OF INDIA IN ONE YEAR
27. EAT AT A 5-STAR
28. EAT AT A *DHABA*
29. SEE THE SEVEN WONDERS OF THE WORLD
30. GO TO DISNEYLAND
31. TRAVEL WHOLE INDIA
32. DO VOLANTEER WORK
33. DONATE 1% OF YOUR SALARY EVERY MONTH
34. ATTEND WEDDINGS OF EVERY CULTURE
35. CAMP
36. LEARN DIFFERENT LANGUAGE
37. JUMP OFF THE CLIFF

38. REPRESNT AT THE UN
39. COOK A 7-COURSE MEAL
40. GO DOLPHIN WATCHING
41. LEARN TO PLAY A MUSIC INTRUMENT
42. OPEN A *FRIENDS* THEMED RESTAURANT
43. WORK WITH YOUR IDOL
44. SHOP FROM PARIS
45. VISIT LAHORE
46. WRITE A FAN LETTER
47. SEE THE NORTHERN LIGHTS
48. START AN NGO
49. MAKE YOUR KID WATCH ALL THE 90s CARTOONS
50. SPEAK OUT ABOUT YOUR SEXUAL ASSAULT
51. PERFORM WITH A LIVE BAND
52. DESIGN YOUR OWN COSTUME
53. TOP IN A SUBJECT
54. RECEIVE SOMEONE WITH A BIG WELCOME BOARD ON THE AIRPORT
55. DANCE WITHOUT HESITATION
56. TAKE A LOT OF GROUP PHOTOS
57. MAKE A SCRAPBOOK
58. TAKE DIFFERENT CLASSES
59. KARAOKE

60. GET A GOOD ROUTINE
61. WRITE KIND NOTES AND LEAVE THEM AT RANDOM PLACES
62. HAVE A SPRITUAL PLAYLIST
63. HAVE A TRAVEL PLAYLIST
64. PRAY FOR THE WORLD EVERYDAY
65. GO TO A COSTUME PARTY
66. SPONSER SOMEONE'S EDUCATION
67. ADOPT A CHILD
68. GIFT RANDOM
69. SPEND TIME ALONE WITHOUT PHONE AND PEOPLE
70. PAINT YOUR WALLS
71. READ 100 BOOKS OF DIFFERENT GENRE
72. WRITE YOUR STORY AND GET IS PUBLISHED
73. CREATE A MINI FOREST IN YOUR GARDEN
74. HAVE A GARDEN
75. PLAY FOR MONEY
76. PLAY LAWN TENNIS
77. DO 50 SETS OF SURYANAMASKAR DAILY
78. PLANT A VEGETABLE GARDEN
79. PUBLISH 50 MEANINGFUL BLOG POSTS
80. LEARN SPORTS
81. BUILD A TREE HOUSE
82. GO TO BED WITHOUT PHONE

83. GO TO AN AWESOME CONCERT
84. BEAT AN EVE TEASER ON ROAD
85. TAKE A POTTERY CLASS
86. HAVE A BOOK LAUNCH
87. RELEASE YOUR SONG
88. HAVE A HEALTHY EATING PLAN
89. BUY A GOOD CAMERA.
90. MAKE VLOGS ON SOMETHING COMMON YET UNCOMMOM
100. TAKE FULL RESPONSIBILITY OF PARENTS WITHOUT INTERFERING IN THEIR LIFE

Not To Dos

1. Mindless scrolling
2. Not Knowing yourself
3. Not trying to change that bothers you
4.Trying to change people that are out of your control
5.Not letting go of the past
6.Not forgiving yourself
7.Forgiving yourself easily
8.Overusing the phone
9.Not drinking enough water
10.Living in a toxic relationship for the sake of nostalgia

Reading Bucketlist

1.Comics

2.Award winner

3. Simple YA

4.Drama

5.Book turned into movie

6.New writer

7.Classics

8.Your favorite author

9.Your favorite book

10.Biography

11.Autobiography

12.Friend's recommendation

13.Disturbing book

14.Psycho thriller

15.Book with more than 1000 pages

Bonus read:- Dear Future Husband (Link in author's page)

Notes

www.ingramcontent.com/pod-product-compliance
Lightning Source LLC
LaVergne TN
LVHW050428160726
843469LV00041B/1279

* 9 7 8 9 3 5 4 3 8 3 9 0 8 *